FINDER'S FEE

Monday

Templeton saw the dog as soon as he switched off the car. He sighed, pulled his keys from the ignition, grabbed his briefcase and got out, hoping the animal would run off. Instead, it wagged its tail. Templeton slammed the car door far harder than usual, but that didn't do any good either. He drew a deep breath, and then walked swiftly toward the dog, swinging his briefcase.

"Go on!" Templeton shouted. "Go on, get out of here!" The dog lowered its head, but stayed put.

He didn't recognize the breed. A mutt of some kind. Gray and white shorthair of medium size, not like any of the other dogs in the neighborhood, all of whom were kept on leashes—short leashes were always best—or behind fences.

This one was lost. The dog was clean and evidently well-fed, but lacked a collar.

PRAISE FOR FINDER'S FEE

"An ice-cold antidote to heart-warming stories."

—MARIO ACEVEDO, author of the Felix Gomez series

PRAISE FOR LUNA ONE

"A tale more chilling than the surface of the moon."

—KEITH FERRELL, *New York Times* bestselling author

"The ending is, literally, explosive, touching and utterly human."

—MARK STEVENS, *Denver Post* bestselling author

These stories are works of fiction. All the characters, organizations, and events portrayed are products of the author's imagination or are used fictitiously.

FINDER'S FEE / LUNA ONE (DOUBLE FEATURE)

Cover design by Colton Hoerner and Joshua Viola

Finder's Fee cover illustration by Damonza.com

Luna One cover illustration by Aaron Lovett

Edited by Mario Acevedo, Keith Ferrell and Matthew Wayne Selznick (MWS Media)

Interior art by Branden Bendert and Aaron Lovett

Typesets and formatting by J.T. Evans

A Hex Publishers Book

Published & Distributed by Hex Publishers, LLC

PO BOX 298

Erie, CO 80516

www.HexPublishers.com

Joshua Viola, Publisher

ISBN-13: 978-1-7339177-9-7

Hex Edition: 2020

Finder's Fee previously published in *Found* (RMFW Press) 2016, ed. Mario Acevedo

Luna One previously published by Hex Publishers, LLC 2014

10 9 8 7 6 5 4 3 2 1

HEX PUBLISHERS
DOUBLE FEATURE

FINDER'S FEE

LUNA ONE

JOSHUA VIOLA

"Get out of here!" Templeton said again, swinging the briefcase high.

The dog didn't get the message—or if it did, it knew Templeton wasn't the sort of guy to swat an animal. Templeton slowly lowered the briefcase and shook his head.

"You're not coming in. And I'm not feeding you."

The dog moved aside as Templeton climbed the two steps that led to the back door. He went into the house, not giving the animal a chance to sneak inside.

***

The dog remained on Templeton's mind all evening, distracting him from his Monday dinner—chicken noodle soup and a grilled cheese sandwich, on the stove at 7:00 and the table at 7:20, each Monday except this one. He burned the first sandwich and wasn't able to eat until 7:25.

It didn't matter. Templeton's appetite was spoiled by the nagging thought that maybe the dog would like the leftovers, or even the burned sandwich. He pushed the thoughts away. The worst thing he could do was feed a stray, especially a well-behaved stray that continued to sit politely on his stoop.

Tuesday

When the alarm clock went off at precisely 6:15 Tuesday morning, Templeton was surprised he had slept. He hadn't expected to. He went through his wakeup motions and took no effort to see if the dog was still outside. Doing that would mean breaking his routine, and that was not going to happen again.

He put himself through the paces of his morning shower and shave, then back into the bedroom to dress in his Tuesday suit, shirt, and tie. Only when his perfectly polished shoes were laced did he go to the kitchen for breakfast. Not once did he look out the back door.

Nor did he so much as glance in that direction as he washed and put away his dishes. Only when he opened the door did he see the dog, still sitting patiently in the same spot. Templeton went outside, descended the steps and walked to his car.

The interior of the vehicle was already warm from the morning sun. It was going to be a hot one. Templeton started the car, but before he turned on the air conditioning, he looked back at the dog and then his watch.

Templeton sighed and shut off the ignition. He sprinted to the shed, retrieved a bucket, filled it with water and placed it on the stoop with just enough time left to avoid morning traffic.

***

Templeton stole a few minutes during his lunch to surf the local missing and found pet sites on the Web. None of the pictures or descriptions bore any resemblance to the dog.

As he worked his way through the afternoon's stack of files, Templeton, more than once, considered calling Animal Control, but stopped short of that when he realized there'd probably be paperwork-complaint forms and the like. He didn't need that sort of disruption in his life.

Disruption, he thought a couple times during the afternoon. The word returned to him as he drove home where, no surprise really, he found the dog on the stoop, wagging its tail as Templeton got out of the car.

"Disruptor," Templeton said. "Is that your name, boy? It's sure a good one for you."

The dog wagged its tail.

"All right, Disruptor, you just sit there. I'm going in the house to get on with my evening. Sit there all night for all I care." He made a stern face.

But before he went into the house, Templeton filled the water bucket again. And when he fixed his Tuesday dinner of French bread pizza, he toasted an extra half loaf and tossed it into the backyard.

Wednesday

Templeton did every bit of his grocery shopping on Saturdays, from 8:45 to 9:45 in the morning. He kept a well-stocked pantry and freezer, the inventory maintained by detailed lists, meticulously kept. He never once ran out of anything essential, never once had any reason to go to the supermarket other than Saturday morning.

But Templeton made an exception just this once and stopped at the grocery store on his way home from work for dog food. He drew the line, though, at buying any kind of dish for the animal, and fed Disruptor his next meal on a paper plate.

Thursday

On Thursday morning, Templeton took pictures of Disruptor. He thought of using them to make a *FOUND DOG* flyer and posting it on Craigslist, in store windows, and on telephone poles around town. He supposed he could do that over the weekend, maybe on Sunday. As long as the dog remained well-behaved, there didn't seem to be any hurry.

That night, he prepared an extra meal and sat on the stoop beside Disruptor. Templeton was pleased when the dog nuzzled him once the paper plate was clean. He put an arm around his guest and they sat together as the light faded.

Friday

Templeton took a longer lunch hour than usual and spent it in a pet store. He bought some toys, food and water dishes, and a collar and leash. A dog as good as Disruptor was bound to have people looking for him and Templeton knew he'd need the proper equipment to take the dog home.

And if nobody called—he figured he'd give it four or five days, a week at most—it wouldn't hurt to have a leash around anyway. Plus, Templeton realized, it wasn't right for a dog as good as Disruptor to have to eat his meals from paper plates.

Saturday

Templeton got his Saturday shopping done in less than half an hour, close to record time, and came home with some dog treats along with his groceries.

He rearranged his normal schedule in order to spend much of the day outside. He mowed the lawn–Disruptor wasn't scared of the mower, but kept a safe distance, walking behind Templeton as he cut the grass. The dog came closer as Templeton pruned the shrubbery, and followed him as he gathered up the trimmings and took them to the trashcan. Disruptor picked up a branch from one of the piles and walked beside his new friend, repeating the act until the job was done.

"Thanks, boy. You're a good helper, yes you are," Templeton said, leaning down and rubbing Disruptor's head. He considered letting the dog come inside while he checked his way through everything else that needed to be done. After a second thought, though, he decided he wasn't quite ready to clean dog messes from the carpet.

Templeton paused for a minute, then made two slow circuits of the yard, Disruptor walking patiently beside him. He found no evidence that the dog had done his business anywhere in the area. He would have seen Disruptor's droppings when he mowed, or worse, stepped in them. But there was nothing. The yard was immaculate.

"Where you going to the bathroom, boy?" Templeton said to Disruptor when they returned to the back stoop. Disruptor climbed the steps and took up his customary position.

They sat together for a few minutes. Templeton occasionally reached out to scratch Disruptor's ears. When he finally went into the house to get on with the day's tasks, he held the door open. Disruptor entered slowly, and spent a few minutes sniffing here and there.

"It's okay, boy," Templeton said. "You just make yourself at home. I've got some things to do, but I'll be right here if you need me." He would have sworn Disruptor smiled at him, and he petted the dog before heading to the laundry room. Disruptor didn't follow, and when Templeton returned, he found the dog curled in a corner, sound asleep.

***

Saturdays were cookout nights, and Templeton made an extra hamburger patty for Disruptor, who ate it happily and rubbed against the cook's legs when it was gone. Templeton thought about letting him come into the house for the night, but why tempt fate?

They'd had a good day together, and tomorrow, once the flyers were made and posted, he would let him come inside again. If that went well, maybe he would fix a place for him to sleep in the living room.

Unless the flyers worked and the owners got in touch.

The thought bothered Templeton, and he decided to ignore it until the time came. He gave Disruptor an extra pat on the head before he retired for the night.

"I'll see you in the morning, boy," he said, and left the dog outside.

Sunday

When Templeton stepped out the back door with a bag of kibble, the stoop was empty.

Disruptor was gone.

Templeton caught his breath, startled by the sadness washing through him. How could such a small dog leave such a large, empty place on the stoop?

What happened to him? Had he run off in search of another stoop? Maybe he got hit on one of the roads that ran through the neighborhood. Some of them were high traffic, and people drove far too fast. Or maybe Animal Control picked him up. Templeton realized he had no idea what Disruptor did after dark and wished he'd brought him inside. Once he bought the food and water dishes, he *should have* brought him inside.

At least he had photos, Templeton thought, the ones he was going to use to make a flyer (and plenty more he would keep once Disruptor's rightful owners reclaimed their pet).

It struck Templeton then, forcefully, that he could still make a flyer; only this one would be a *LOST DOG* flyer, with Disruptor's picture, contact information, and promise of a reward. It would be worth a reward, even a healthy one, to get the dog back.

He turned to go into the house and get to work, but as he opened the door, he caught a glimpse of something coming through the hedge at the far end of his backyard.

Templeton dropped the bag of food and raced down the steps, falling to his knees on grass still damp with dew, and called, "Disruptor!"

The dog had something in his mouth, and for a moment, gave no indication of hearing Templeton.

Templeton called louder, "Disruptor! What you got there, boy? Where you been?"

Disruptor spun toward him, tail high and wagging fast as he bounded across the yard, the treasure still held in his mouth. The dog dropped the item in midstride and ran faster.

Templeton held out his arms, and Disruptor came into them at full speed, nearly knocking him over. Only after a moment of playful wrestling did Templeton let Disruptor go. The dog returned to the item he'd dropped, picking it up in his teeth, and brought it eagerly—*proudly*—for inspection.

Templeton realized what it was even before Disruptor released it into his hands. He didn't want to look.

It was a dog collar, a well-worn one, just Disruptor's size, with a scuffed metal tag bearing an address.

***

It was late in the morning and he'd put it off long enough. Templeton didn't have any trouble getting Disruptor into the car. The dog hopped up on the passenger seat.

Templeton waited a while before putting the car in gear. They had a good drive ahead of them. The address was on Route 26, a ways out in the country. It would've been a lot easier if there had been a phone number or a vet's name or anything else on the tag, anything that might have saved him the drive to take Disruptor home. But there was nothing, only the address—21.7 miles away.

"You came a long way, boy, didn't you?" Templeton said as he backed slowly out of his driveway. "How'd you happen to come that far? And to come all that way to me? Is that what you did, Disruptor? Come all that way just for me? Well, I'm glad you did, I'm glad it was me you found."

Disruptor's tail thumped on the upholstery.

Templeton drove slowly, maintaining his speed when they left the city and headed into farmland. "You a farm dog, boy?" he said when the odometer showed they'd reached the halfway point. The thought made Templeton feel good—a dog like Disruptor needed wide-open spaces to run and play.

Into the last five miles of the drive, Disruptor moved close to Templeton and rested his head on the man's shoulder. Templeton nearly turned the car around right then, but the jingling collar told him to keep going.

They reached the address, identified by faded numbers on the side of a battered mailbox atop a slanted post. Beside the mailbox was a narrow and rutted dirt path that led through a pine thicket with various *NO TRESPASSING: VIOLATORS WILL BE SHOT* signs on display.

Templeton decided he didn't want to drive down the road, and as he began to pass it, Disruptor sat straight, looking through the driver's side window, right at the mailbox and the dirt driveway that disappeared into the pines.

Disruptor moved his forepaws onto Templeton's lap and pressed his muzzle against the window. His tail wagged furiously, and for the first time in their week together, Templeton heard Disruptor bark.

It was a *great* bark.

"All right, boy," he said, and took his right hand from the wheel to hold him close. "You're right, this is where you belong. I'll take you home."

He stopped the car, backed up a bit, and turned onto the narrow road, taking it slow all the way. The drive emerged from the pines and entered a broad clearing, an old two-story house with a wide front porch at its center.

Disruptor barked on the way to the edge of the house's yard, where Templeton parked beside a beat-up pickup truck.

"You brought him home!" said an old man who came to the door even before Templeton and the dog were out of the car. "You brought home my Finder!"

Finder, Templeton thought. *Nice name, but nowhere near as good as Disruptor.*

The dog strained at the leash and pulled Templeton from the car onto the porch. He bounded up the steps and into the arms of the old man who was leaning down to welcome him home.

"Finder, you good dog! Looks like you did it again, didn't you?"

"Here, let me help you with that," Templeton said, reaching to unhook the leash. He gently brushed his knuckles against Disruptor's muzzle and looked into the dog's happy eyes. He wondered if his own eyes looked sad.

Disruptor didn't move away when the leash was unhooked. He might be Finder, but he stayed close to the man who'd given him his new name. Templeton put an arm around the dog and rubbed his head.

"I don't have much in the way of a reward," the old man said softly.

"No, no," Templeton said. "I couldn't, *wouldn't* take anything. I'm just glad he's home."

"Well, I am too," the man said. "But would you at least have a glass of iced tea? It's not much, but we'd be happy—we'd be pleased, Finder and me, if you'd come in for a glass."

Templeton shook his head. "I really should be going." It wouldn't be easy to leave Disruptor behind, and the longer he stayed, the harder it would get.

"Please, won't you?" the old man said. "Finder and I would like you to sit with us for a bit. I'll tell you how he got his name."

What Templeton wanted, suddenly and deeply, was to sit with Disruptor on his back stoop again, just sit there with the dog close to him. He was going to miss him.

"All right," Templeton said. "A quick glass of tea would be nice."

***

The interior of the house was crowded and cluttered with furniture whose best days were at least a generation behind them. But the place appeared to be clean, and Templeton couldn't deny that Disruptor–*Finder*–was happy to be here. The dog danced twice around Templeton's legs as they entered the living room, then bounded across the threadbare carpet and through an open door into the kitchen, where claws skittered on the linoleum floor.

"You just have a seat right there," the man said, "and I'll get us some tea." He followed the dog into the kitchen. Templeton heard a refrigerator open, ice being added to glasses.

While the man fetched the tea, Disruptor came back into the room and sat directly in front of Templeton. He leaned forward and petted the dog. "I'm gonna miss you, boy," he whispered. "I'm gonna miss you a lot."

He felt sure Disruptor understood him and saw a similar sentiment in the dog's eyes.

The man came back into the room. "Finder, don't you bother our guest, not when he's gone to so much trouble for you."

"It was no trouble at all," Templeton said, and meant it. He took a glass from the man, pleased to see it was spotless, and drank. The tea was good, sweet and tart, with just the right bite.

"You'll have to pardon our housekeeping," the man said as he seated himself opposite Templeton. "It's just Finder and me here, and we don't get much company. Sure was lonely while he was gone."

"It's fine," Templeton said, taking another long swallow. He thought about how lonely his own house would be when he got home.

"Well, you're kind to say so," the man said. "It suits Finder and me anyways, this place. We do all right here by ourselves."

"He's a good dog," Templeton said, eager to finish his tea and be gone—to go and leave Disruptor behind and get back to his routines. He felt sadness gathering within him, and something else, deeper than sadness. He looked at

Disruptor, sitting patiently in a corner of the room, tail wagging, those wide eyes of his watching him as he took another drink. "He's a great dog."

The old man chuckled.

"Fell for him, did you?" he said, and didn't wait for Templeton to answer. "Thought so, they all did, every one of them."

Every one of whom? Templeton thought, but didn't say out loud. His tongue suddenly felt thick and his lips a little numb. Templeton's eyes watered and grew heavy. He bit down against a yawn.

"Every one of my Finders over the years—every one of 'em—got their people to fall flat in love with them. But I'll tell you now, this one's the best of them all. I'd work him harder, send him out more often to do his finding, but about one a year is all that really feels safe. He'd sure like more than that, wouldn't you, Finderboy? He's got a way of finding just the right people."

Templeton heard the dog's tail thumping against the floor as the old man continued.

"It's like he can sense them." The old man's voice sounded like echoes in a long tunnel. "Something about my Finder lets him sense just the right ones. The lonely ones, most of them. Good people, no doubt, but not good enough to have anybody to miss them. That sound familiar? I bet it does. Doesn't that sound just like him, Finderboy?"

Templeton turned his head to look at the dog, sure that tail would be wagging. He felt like his neck was wrapped in concrete. His eyelids tried to drift down and he struggled to find the energy to keep them open. He forced himself to lean forward, willing his right hand to reach for the glass. Maybe another jolt of cold tea would wake him up.

But the old man beat him to it.

"You don't need any more of that," he said, taking the glass from the table beside Templeton. "You've had just enough, just the right amount. Any more and it gets into the meat. Don't it, Finderboy?"

Templeton couldn't keep his eyes open any longer, and knew if he closed them, he'd never open them again.

The last thing Templeton saw, the final break in his routine, was Finder—*Disruptor*—sitting patiently in the corner, tail wagging happily as he licked his chops.

LUNA ONE

If you could see the Earth illuminated when you were in a place as dark as night, it would look to you more splendid than the Moon.
—Galileo

Eddie still thought of it as full gravity, Earth-normal.

More than thirty years after his last space flight—closer to forty if he cared to be honest about it, which he didn't—Eddie still couldn't admit that the planet where he and every other member of the human race had been born was where he was going to die. Here, in full gravity, Earth-normal. As if any other kind was available to him.

Eddie could feel the Moon laughing at him.

It was one of those afternoons he hated, the Moon out in daylight, pale and almost translucent, but still the Moon, and no question about it. And no question it was laughing.

He downshifted, and his old truck strained and shuddered as it tried to make the same grade it used to make without much effort. Hell, Eddie and his truck used to fly up this very hill. What did gravity mean then? Something you could push against, and if you pushed hard enough, you could outrun it.

Push hard enough, Eddie thought as his truck coughed and complained and shed more speed, and you could outrun it all the way to the Moon. Two dozen others pushed it that hard. All managed to circle the Moon, and a dozen of them walked on it before coming back here, to full gravity.

Earth-normal.

Should have been thirty-three who made the trip, which would have meant sixteen humans would have walked on lunar soil. One of those sixteen would have been Eddie. But Apollo 20 got canned the same way 18 and 19 got canned—all the training, money, hopes and dreams, every last bit of the manned lunar landing program canned for budget politics, and Eddie along with it.

The essence of Eddie, anyway. The heart of him, the Big Dream he had since he was a kid was the only sort of dream worth having, the only thing he could ever remember wishing for. The Moon, and him standing upon it.

NASA had tossed him a crumb or two. He got his shuttle missions, made his flights, did two spacewalks, got to work and float and sleep and wake above the Earth, free from gravity.

Except he wasn't, really. Just a couple hundred miles above the hill his truck fought against right now, that was as far as the shuttle went. Not much farther than the driving distance from Canaveral to Miami. Not far enough.

Not nearly far enough to really be free of gravity.

It was always there, pulling on the shuttle, drawing it back every second of the mission. Eddie could feel it. Even in his spacesuit outside the shuttle, floating, he could feel it—clutching at him, tugging on him, pulling him back.

He jammed the sole of his foot harder against the gas pedal, but the pedal didn't have anywhere to go, no more than the old truck's engine had any more to give. Still, Eddie pushed.

The worst of it, up there, floating, had been the Moon. He could see it when he took his walk. Brighter than ever without any atmosphere between him and it, big enough that he could touch it. And he would have if he could have reached. But he never could, and the Moon laughed at him, up there, as he floated.

Eddie still heard that laughter, even over the groans and creaks and stuttering cough of his truck. Over the ringing in his ears that got louder and louder as he got madder and madder. He could even hear it over the sudden honking and jeers from the car full of kids that came up behind his truck. The car pulled out and sped around him, its windows down and the kids leaning their bodies out into the wind as they flaunted their youth.

"Spaceman!" they shouted. They would have seen the NASA ASTRONAUT and SHUTTLE CREW stickers on his bumper, faded and tattered and barely clinging to the rusted metal, but still hanging on to be read… and mocked.

"Get off the road and get yourself a rocket ship, spaceman! Blast off, grandpa!"

One of them stuck his bare ass out the window and spread his cheeks as the others shouted, "Moon, man!"

Eddie closed his eyes for just a second and pushed harder on the gas, half wishing for the kids, their shiny, fast car and their youth to find out exactly what gravity was. How hard it could pull. What it could do if there was another car, or, even better and far more certain, a big-rig carrying a full load coming up the other side of the hill, timed perfectly to smash its mass straight-on into theirs. How much time would the kids have to turn their jeers and taunts into screams and death rattles?

But wishes didn't come true. If they did, Eddie's footprints would be on the Moon… and the road ahead of the kids wouldn't be so clear. By the time the truck made it over the crest, the car was a dot in the distance, moving fast, pushing hard.

Eddie raised his foot from the gas pedal and let the truck relax and roll, all straining past. The vibrations dwindled. The desiccated, rocket-shaped air freshener that hung from the rearview gradually ceased its gyrations and settled into a steady pendulum, back-and-forth, dancing just a bit when Eddie shifted.

That was the last hill between his place and the store, and the only bad one. From here on it was downhill all the way.

***

Eddie pulled open the door of Eleanor's Surplus Warehouse and, as always, a wave of heat caused him to break out in a sweat. Eleanor's air conditioner was as useless as the broken security camera in the back corner of the store.

"Mornin', Eddie," said a middle-aged woman with a wide, partially toothless grin.

Eddie tipped his hat and walked by without making eye contact. "Eleanor."

He moved through the crowded racks of merchandise to the back of the building, eyes closed, walking the same path he walked every Wednesday afternoon. A test he made himself take once a week just to prove he could still pass it.

He often wondered if Eleanor would rearrange the aisles or introduce a new endcap of product that would send him tumbling to the ground—an accident that might end with a broken arm or leg. To some extent, he hoped so. He longed for change. For excitement. For something… new. Something that would add some flavor to his life.

Eddie moved forward three steps, hearing the familiar sounds of his shoes on bare concrete. Eyes still closed, he turned left behind a rack of first aid kits, took six more paces and—a deep, low howl filled the store. Eddie snapped his eyes open. He saw other customers watching, unable to resist the spectacle at the back of the warehouse.

"Kali!" Eleanor hollered.

Eddie looked down and saw his right foot planted on the tail of a Golden Retriever.

"Whatcha doin' to my dog, Eddie?"

He lifted his heel and the dog whimpered away.

"Why don't you keep her on a leash?" Eddie said under his breath, embarrassed by the attention projected on him. He turned around and nearly fell into a rack stocked with flare guns. He regained his balance fast and pulled one of the packages from a metal display arm, reading the label to help hide his humiliation.

Can reach an altitude up to 500 feet with the brightness of 16,000 candles.

Eddie imagined himself pointing the gun at the rowdy teenager's bare ass that mooned him on the way to the store. He smiled, placed it back on the display, and continued down the aisles.

After a few more shortcuts through the maze of products, Eddie arrived at his destination. He scanned a familiar wall of freeze-dried space food. Caramel apples, strawberries and ice cream. Everything but the flavor he came for, black beans and rice. He let out a frustrated groan and piled a few packets into his arms.

He only purchased freeze-dried food, a habit he picked up during his time in mission training, and he only purchased them here. He rarely ventured to other retail outlets. He hated grocery stores, the crowds of people, the squalling children, the armies of clerks and stockers and managers, all insisting on being helpful no matter how often he said he didn't want it.

Eleanor's didn't have much, but it had everything he needed. The two or three customers here beat the large crowds at the Wal-Mart a few miles up the road. He returned to the counter with his purchases.

"You're extra friendly today, aren't ya?" Eleanor said.

"You're out of black beans and rice."

She chuckled, "You're the only one who buys that stuff, y'know? Not much demand for it." She punched some numbers into the register and placed the items in a paper bag. "Been following news of that Moon mission? Right up your alley, ain't it? Got that ast'roid flyby coming in soon, too—you gonna watch that on that 'scope of yours?"

Eddie replied with no more than a slight wince and dug his right hand into the pocket of his NASA windbreaker. "See to having black beans and rice next Wednesday. I can't live on caramel apples and ice cream."

Eleanor rolled her eyes as Eddie tossed a wad of crumpled bills and coins on the counter and left.

***

After NASA dumped him, more than three decades ago, Eddie poured his life savings into a twenty-acre farm in northern Virginia. The little farmhouse sat on the tallest hill in the area and offered the clearest view of the midnight sky. A large telescope, nearly a third the size of the home, jutted from the rooftop like a cannon.

The interior was immaculate. Posters from Russia, China, the US, and half a dozen private space ventures covered every open wall of the house. Paintings, photographs, schematics from various projects from around the world, new and old, alive and dead, were on display. Model shuttles and rockets hung from fishing line attached to the ceiling and ran the length of the hallway that led to the kitchen. A mockup of Earth's moon sat upon a mantle in the dining room. A library of astronomy books lined the shelves to either side of the fireplace.

Eddie set his keys on the kitchen table and organized the supplies he'd purchased. He placed the packets of food inside specially labeled cupboards above the sink.

He was nearly done when a rhythmic thud echoed through the hallway from the front door. Eddie ignored it, but the knocking came again. He cursed under his breath and went to answer the door.

A young boy, no more than thirteen, stood in the entryway. Dressed in a school uniform, the boy stared up at him. Eddie looked beyond the child and saw a bicycle propped against his truck.

"Good afternoon, sir," the boy said.

"They don't make kickstands nowadays? Sure hope that bike of yours didn't scratch my truck."

The boy stepped forward, ignoring the comment, and handed Eddie a catalog. "My name is David Lovett and I'm a student at Westlake Middle School. We're selling Virginia's world-famous peanuts. A portion of the proceeds will go to a college fund for the top ten students in my graduating class."

The rehearsed words nearly made Eddie choke, but he took the catalog.

"Your generosity will allow me to achieve my dreams," the boy continued, "and make my wishes come true."

A scowl crept across Eddie's face. Without raising his eyes from the catalog, he said, "Take it from me, kid, dreams don't come true."

He tossed the brochure back at David and shut the door.

Generosity. What a joke.

Nobody had ever been generous to Eddie. He worked his way up the ladder, spent decades of his life—even sacrificed his marriage—only to be let go from a program he helped develop. He'd wished for the Moon, dreamed of it… and got fired for his troubles. If life taught Eddie anything, it was that generosity was as impossible as his dream of walking on lunar soil.

Soon, somebody else would have their wish fulfilled, for the first time since the Seventies. And whoever that was, the only thing that mattered to Eddie was that it wasn't him.

He stepped into the living room and switched on the TV. A news broadcast taunted him with its lead story: the pending announcement of the private mission to place a human on the Moon. More than that—to place a permanent resident on the Moon.

Luna One Corporation's plans for its manned mission to the Moon are nearly complete. The selection process is finished, the candidates, whose names have been kept secret from the public, have been gathered for the announcement of the individual selected. The name of the lunanaut—as they call them—will be announced at a press conference tomorrow morning.

Eddie watched the broadcast for no more than a minute before switching it off. He was about to take his usual place in his recliner, positioned in the middle of the room directly beneath the massive telescope he had custom-mounted with a rooftop dome, when he glimpsed his daughter's face among a cluster of framed photos and memorabilia on a nearby shelf.

He stopped, reached for it, then, scowling, reached instead for a framed letter propped behind it. He clenched his teeth. The letter, printed with an official Luna One logo, read:

It is with sincere regret that we must inform you that your application for the Luna One project has been declined.

Why in hell had he framed this?

He knew why. It was a reminder of just what he was worth to the Moon. Nothing. Less than nothing. He was stuck here, and he would die here.

His fingers closed tightly on the frame. If he could have found the person who sent that letter, he would have killed him right then. Eddie tossed the frame back at the shelving and knocked the photo of his daughter to the floor. The glass inside the frame shattered.

Wishes. Wish all you want and you still have broken pieces to pick up.

All Eddie ever wished for was the Moon, to stand upon it. Not to be an old man with glass to sweep up.

He felt a sudden dizziness and ringing gathered in his ears.

Eddie staggered to the recliner. The old chair groaned as he sat down. Ignoring an unfamiliar stiffness in his chest, he leaned forward and positioned himself below the telescope's large eyepiece. He twisted a set of knobs on the side of the device until an object in space coalesced into focus. He turned another knob, zooming in on the base erected on lunar soil.

"Luna One," he said to himself, but had trouble forming the words. He took a deep breath and fought the anger and the pain swelling inside of him. "Bastards. They should be prepping for me. For the announcement of my name!"

Beads of sweat gathered on his forehead and his heart raced.

"It should be me."

His head sank between his shoulders and he placed his hands over his face, clearing his throat as the rapid thumping of his heart sped at a jogger's pace.

"It ought to be me," he said raggedly, almost gasping for breath.

His hands shook and the Moon grew blurry.

"All I ever wished for, the only wish, was to be… there."

Eddie collapsed.

***

If this is death, Eddie thought, I can live with it.

Thought.

If I can think, how can I be dead?

And with that, panic came. The ringing in his ears became a roar, the pressure on his chest heavy. He wasn't dead yet, but he was dying. He knew he was dying.

He tried to open his eyes, but they remained closed. He tried to raise a hand to his face, but his hand would not respond. His muscles refused to obey his commands. The roaring in his ears grew louder, the pressure on his chest, more intense. He couldn't breathe. Eddie felt a surge of mounting, unstoppable horror.

Stroke.

That's what this was. A stroke, hitting him hard and roaring in his ears as his brain tore itself apart. Desperately, reaching out for any scrap he could hold onto, any iota of himself, his thoughts, his personality, his memories, his dreams, his…life. Eddie pushed himself to…

Think.

More than that, to…

Remember.

But remember what?

He tried to cast his mind back, to find his most recent memory. The assholes taunting him from their car… Eleanor's… Home… His models and schematics… The kid selling peanuts… His daughter's photo… The rejection letter… The telescope… The sky… The asteroid in the news…

The last thing he remembered before the stroke:

The—

Moon.

Eddie wished for the Moon and it killed him. Or, worse, the wish and the Moon came together to destroy him. That had to be what this was. A ravage and a rupture within his brain that would leave him trapped within himself forever.

How could the Moon have done this to him?

Then the largest slam of all stuck him midchest and he woke up. He could breathe again, though the air tasted odd. The roaring was gone and he could hear again, even if all he heard was his own breathing… and his name being called, distantly, again and again, as though someone was trying to rouse him.

Who?

A doctor?

More likely an EMT crew, calling to him as he lay on the floor immobilized by a stroke, dying of a heart attack? Another thought came to him—had he tried to reach the phone? He must have dialed 9-1-1 before he blacked out.

"Eddie. Eddie. Talk to us, Eddie."

He tried to answer, but couldn't. He had to show them a sign. Let them know he heard them.

Feeling was returning to his extremities. His feet were cold, but he could wiggle his toes. Did they see that? Probably not—he was wearing shoes, heavy ones, heavier than the sneakers he'd put on this morning.

"Eddie!" The voice was more anxious. "Eddie, come back!"

They were losing him!

Raise a hand, Eddie told himself.

He couldn't.

Wiggle a finger, then, raise a thumbs-up, hell, give them the finger. Anything to let them know he was here. Still here. He pressed his fingertips against—he wasn't sure what the surface was; it felt familiar but strange, like he was wearing gloves.

"Eddie!" There was fear and urgency in the voice now.

He gulped air, searching for his voice. The air still tasted funny, but it was familiar. He knew the taste, but couldn't remember where he knew it from.

The floor beneath him—or was he still in his recliner? He felt now as though he was sitting—gave a lurch. Eddie felt his body trying to float up. Was he feeling himself leaving his body, floating into death?

He brought every bit of his being—whatever, he thought, was left of it—to bear on getting his eyes open. But they wouldn't obey him. He was trapped in darkness.

"Eddie!"

He arched his back, and felt his body respond. He could finally move. He wiggled his fingers.

"Eddie! Eddie!"

He had to show them more. Eddie swiftly raised his right hand—that would show them that he was alive. That he was, an old phrase came back to him from decades ago, system functional.

"Eddie… you've got us worried!"

But he raised his hand. What were they worried about?

Unless he only imagined raising his hand. A lie from the stroke that was killing his brain. Had he raised his hand or not? One way to find out. He would slap himself, as hard as he could. If that didn't show them, and himself, nothing would.

Holding his breath—what was that taste in the air?—Eddie clasped the fingers of his left hand around his right wrist, splayed the fingers of his right hand and, without further hesitation, brought his palm up hard toward his face.

He almost made it.

His hand slapped a barrier, hard like glass or plastic, and the shock of the impact opened Eddie's eyes. He saw his hand, gloved, directly before him, his palm resting against the transparent surface of what could only be the faceplate of a helmet. Beyond his gloved hand, he saw blinking lights, readouts and monitors.

"What the hell?"

He suddenly realized the taste of the air was from oxygen generators. The roaring in his ears from rocket thrusts as engines broke free from gravity. The weight on his chest from the Gs of liftoff and transit from Earth to space.

The voice in his ears—

"Eddie, dammit, come on. Luna One respond. Luna One, respond or we will be forced to abort."

Eddie took his hand from the helmet's faceplate. He looked around and found the viewport in precisely the right spot, just where it had been on the schematics he studied, the model he built.

"Do you copy, Luna One? Come in, Eddie. Come in."

Eddie's thoughts became clear. If this was death, so be it. If this was a vision borne upon the wings of a stroke, fine. But if this was real, if this was a result of his wish—

Get to it!

"Take it easy down there, Control," Eddie said with a calm that was the exact opposite of what he felt.

Over the sudden outburst of cheering from the control center on Earth, Eddie heard his own voice. The astronaut's twang returned to his words for the first time in thirty years or more, and sounded like the most natural thing in the world.

"Didn't mean to give you guys a scare." He oriented himself so he could better study the view and stared at the Earth.

Free, at last.

***

Three days to the Moon, and how they flew by. It made Eddie chuckle.

Nothing to it. Nothing to any of it that he couldn't bluff his way through, fake his way through, navigate his way through. Same as he made his way through Eleanor's crowded aisles without a single misstep, unless an unexpected variable like a dog's tail was introduced.

No dogs or their tails here. No unexpected variables whatsoever. Other than the granting of his wish; the fact of his own presence. He could ignore that, for now. He would have plenty of time to work through what happened to make his wish come true, all the time he needed once the wish was completed and he stood on the moon of his dreams.

For now, he put himself on auto-control, making his way past obstacles and around barriers with his eyes closed.

It was easier, in some ways, than navigating Eleanor's store. If Eddie had no memories of anything between his blackout in the recliner and his awakening in the Luna One capsule, the world had plenty of memories, and Eddie explored them avidly.

News reports, press conferences, feature stories, blogs, photo essays and slide shows, talking head discussions and debates, late night comic routines ("How old is the lunanaut? He started training for the Moon mission before there was a Moon!"), interviews with former colleagues ("Even after they canceled Apollo 20 out from under us, Eddie knew he'd get there somehow."), quickie books (*Aging Astronaut, Ageless Dreams; A Lunanaut Named Eddie*), even talk of movies and mini-series.

In the blink of an eye—the time it took to make a wish—Eddie found himself a global celebrity. The most famous person on the world he was now happily leaving behind, the world whose gravity he was giddily setting himself free of.

Eddie's anointment as the first inhabitant of the Moon captured the imagination of the public. For all the stories that made Eddie grin with their accounts of the "old man" in space who'd never given up on his dream, there were just as many outraged editorials calling his selection a stunt, or irresponsible, or dangerous, or all three. Those stories didn't bother him. He remembered none of the controversy, any more than he remembered the rigorous training. Or the press conference at which his selection was announced. Or the ceremonies at the launch site. Or the two delays that held the launch back from its scheduled liftoff time.

He remembered none of it, and he didn't mind the memory blanks one bit. While there was a certain pleasure to be found in watching the videos or listening to the commentary or even reading the critical editorials and blog posts, his main purpose in perusing the material was to cover himself in conversations with Mission Control. As far as everyone on the world was concerned, Eddie went through the full training program and was completely qualified for the mission.

And somehow, he was. Somehow, when the wish was granted, he was also granted all of the knowledge, experience and skill a lunanaut would need, and that each of the candidates would have studied exhaustively in the months and years before the final selection.

Eddie spent those months and years staring through his telescope, or half concentrating on the Luna One materials he collected, or driving, once a week, to Eleanor's and back. That was the total of his preparation time for where he was now.

But somehow, Eddie knew how to do things that were requested of him. Everything that was requested of him. Adjustments and recordings, calibration of instruments, drills and dry runs, and even some press interviews as he traveled moonward. The interviews he could fake, but there was no faking the precise and sensitive touch required to handle the spacecraft's instrumentation. The patterns and processes he remembered from the schematics he studied and the Luna One simulations he ran on his computer in the farmhouse back—

Home.

The word came into his thoughts more than once, always accompanied by memories of his comfortable farmhouse, or his telescope and spacecraft models, even of Eleanor's toothless chatter.

He was surprised the real thing, the pouches and packets of nourishment available to him in the capsule, didn't taste as good as the ones he bought from her.

It was just a matter of adjustment and getting used to being in space once more. Getting accustomed to weightlessness and the fact that his dream came true. His wish had been granted. It was a lot to take in.

Not that he spent much time thinking about it. There was too much else to do before he landed on his new home, and only three days to get it done.

Among the tasks he most enjoyed was his twice-daily visual check on the asteroid that would make near-Earth passage just after he landed and took up residence in the small quarters waiting for him.

The rock was half the size of Texas, one hell of an asteroid, and its approach to within a quarter of a million miles from Earth—same distance as the Moon—was the astronomical event of the decade, maybe the century. The publicity team at Luna One Corporation lobbied hard for a mission to land a crew on the asteroid, and if there was more time the company—or the Russians or the Chinese—might have pulled that stunt off.

But the asteroid was coming in too fast. So, the publicity team orchestrated a twice-daily asteroid-cam and commentary feed from the capsule to display the closest ever asteroid transit of Earth. Eddie pretty much stuck to the scripts they gave him but managed to add a few of his own touches, including one he worked on for his last commentary before landing.

"It's something to think about, all of you down there in the gravity well," he said. "All the time, knowledge, skill, and hard work it took to break me free of Earth's gravity and send me here… and of how little effort, really, that old rock had to make. It just is, and it just goes. And goes. After I step out onto my new home, that asteroid will whiz by me and the Moon, past you and the Earth, and just keep going. We'll all watch, probably cheer a little, some of you may pray and some raise a glass in toast. But whatever we do or say, the asteroid won't hear, won't care. Makes you think, doesn't it?"

That particular commentary won its share of praise ("Who knew the first lunanaut was also something of a poet and philosopher?") and condemnation ("That asteroid was set in motion by God and it is not for man to speculate on what it does and doesn't care about!") but by that point Eddie was too busy getting ready for the landing and the start of his new life.

When the spacecraft turned over for landing, Eddie was presented with a view of the Earth that spoke to him in ways that he hadn't expected.

Memories. Childhood sunsets, his sixth birthday party and the cake his mother made, his father taking the training wheels off his bicycle, the first time he brought home a straight-A report card, his first car and his first kiss, the first time he soloed in a jet, his first space flight, being selected for Apollo, the first shuttle flight and the slow glide home, the first time he saw his little farm, the first time he used the telescope he installed in his roof, the first time he saw his daughter…

"Beautiful," he said softly, almost afraid his voice would break.

"You got that right, Eddie!" Mission Control said in a cheerful voice. Control was always cheerful, which made Eddie glad he never ran into them on Earth.

"Beautiful all the way down the line, just like you said, Luna One," Control continued. "All systems humming perfectly, everything in absolute order, we'll have you on the surface soon. Right on time to join us in watching the transit."

Eddie relaxed into his seat. Everything was under Control's *control* from here on. In truth, the whole mission could have been automated, but there was publicity advantage—so the corporation said, anyway—to having at least a few things for the lunanaut to do.

Now he had nothing to do but wait and watch the Earth shrink as he dropped toward his new home. Eddie let his memories flow.

He was drifting among those memories when the first short pulse of the landing engines triggered.

"Wake you up?" Control said with a laugh. "Telemetry said you were sleeping or in a trance."

Eddie blinked hard. Maybe he had dozed. Either way, he was back now. The Earth was still there ahead of him, but he lost his angle of view when two more short bursts from the engine adjusted the spacecraft's descent path. That was all right. He would see the Earth again from the surface of the Moon. A whole new perspective, he thought.

Control set the spacecraft down as gently as a caring parent settles an infant into a crib. Eddie felt the vibrations of the long, slow final descent toward the surface. Heard the count-off as Control announced the distance remaining before landing. Luna One's three broad feet made contact with the Moon and Control cut the spacecraft's engines.

"Successful landing and shut down. With a whole half-liter of fuel to spare," Control announced. "We put you down forty meters from your residence, just a short walk to your front door after your commute."

Eddie thought of his pickup truck, forever parked in the yard near the farmhouse.

"Welcome to the Moon, Luna One. Welcome home, Eddie."

Eddie was already unbuckling his safety harnesses, disconnecting the umbilicals that linked him to the spacecraft's systems, checking the seals on his suit, getting himself ready to step outside.

"Slow down," Control said. "Give us just a second to get the cameras adjusted so we can catch your first steps for posterity."

Eddie moved to the spacecraft's hatch and forced himself to wait for a period that seemed longer than the entire voyage.

"All right, Luna One. You are cleared for egress and lunar residence. We're sharing your emergence with the world, so we hope you have something memorable to say."

Eddie had, in fact, been given a script—*In the name of the hopes of humanity and the Luna One Corporation I hereby take up residence on the Moon*—but he had no intention of using those words. He had his own statement to make. After all, what were they going to do? Evict him?

"You are now cleared to open the hatch and step outside," Control said. "Step outside and join the people of Earth as we, and the first of many thousands of lunar residents, watch the transit of the asteroid past our now two inhabited worlds."

The hatch opened and a small ladder extruded from the side of the spacecraft. Eddie backed out of the capsule and descended three of the ladder's four steps, then paused for an instant and drew a breath in preparation for his speech.

There was no point, Eddie had known all along, as had all the others, save one, who preceded him, in trying to equal Armstrong's *one small step*. And so, when he pushed himself from the ladder and settled to the surface, he spoke the truest words he knew, straight from the center of every dream he ever had.

"I made it!"

If Control was disconcerted by Eddie's abandonment of the script the publicity department prepared, they didn't let on. "You certainly did, Eddie. First inhabitant of the Moon, and it's you!"

His helmet filled with raucous, echoing cheers from the crew at Mission Control. He took a step away from the spacecraft and glanced at the small cluster of prefabricated domes that would be his new home. He was pleased to see one of the domes had a telescope protruding from its roof, but almost immediately he turned away from the domes and looked back at Earth.

"I am," Eddie said, "grateful to everyone at Luna One Corporation for making this dream of mine—and of humanity's—come true." The applause continued.

"Eddie, we've got someone here who'd like to speak with you. Patching her through now."

"Dad? Daddy, can you hear me?"

Eddie's eyes widened.

"Marilyn? Oh my God, Lynn, is that you?"

"You did it, Dad! You finally did it. I'm so proud of you!"

It was years since Eddie and his daughter last spoke and far more since they got along. He smiled and said the first thing that came to mind. "I'm sorry. I—"

"Don't. It's okay. You worked so hard for this. You deserve this. And when the shuttles are ready, I'll be on the first one out."

"I'd like that," Eddie said.

The cheering from Mission Control was exuberant and brief.

Eddie kept his grin in place when he heard the whoops, backslaps, laughter and applause all stop. No dwindling, no slow but steady tapering off. The joy just stopped.

"Eddie," Mission Control said, cutting Marilyn's transmission.

"Yes?" he replied, looking around his new home, but looking even more frequently back at the home he left.

"Eddie—God." Something in Control's voice.

"What is it?" Eddie said. He could feel his heartrate rising and his forehead go clammy with sweat. His grin was gone now.

"We have an anomaly."

"What sort of anomaly?"

"It's impossible, what's happened is physically impossible."

"What is?"

"The—the asteroid. It shifted, just now, just as you—"

"What?"

"Just as you stepped onto the Moon it… shifted."

"Shifted how? What are you saying, Control?"

"It's going to… It's going to—"

"Going to what?"

"Hit," Control said.

Eddie felt a flare of panic he fought to contain. "Hit? Hit here? The Moon?" He turned and looked beyond the horizon, toward deeper space, and thought of his daughter.

He couldn't die here. He had to see her again.

"No," Control said. "Not the Moon."

Eddie looked back at the Earth, but already much of the blue planet was obscured by the asteroid.

"Can't you stop it?"

The question had no answer and Control did not attempt to offer one. The noise in Eddie's headphones was that of panic, grief, weeping and prayer.

Eddie stepped farther away from the spacecraft, unable to take his eyes from the thin sliver of earthlight he could see around the asteroid that now eclipsed his view of the planet.

Gradually, but with increasing speed, the disc of the eclipse dwindled, revealing more and more of the Earth and its shimmering beauty to Eddie. He tried to find words, tried to think of something to say to Control. To Marilyn.

A rapidly brightening flare began to form itself around the asteroid. Its transit cut a burning, terminal trail toward…

I should be there, Eddie thought.

He made another wish, the only wish in the universe that mattered now.

"I wish I was home, with Marilyn."

No more than an instant later, he wished he had enough courage to look away. Earth and all of its inhabitants ceased to exist in a cataclysm born of the gravity Eddie would never escape.

ABOUT THE AUTHOR

JOSHUA VIOLA is a four-time Colorado Book Award finalist and co-author of the Denver Moon series with Warren Hammond. His comic book collection, *Denver Moon: Metamorphosis*, was included on the 2018 Bram Stoker Award Preliminary Ballot for Superior Achievement in a Graphic Novel. He edited the *Denver Post* #1 bestselling anthology, *Nightmares Unhinged*, and co-edited *Cyber World*—named one of the best science fiction anthologies of 2016 by Barnes & Noble. His fiction has appeared in numerous anthologies, *Birdy* magazine, and on *Tor.com*. He is owner and chief editor of Hex Publishers.

OTHER BOOKS
BY JOSHUA VIOLA
FROM HEX PUBLISHERS

NOVELS

The Bane of Yoto (with Nicholas Karpuk)

Denver Moon: The Minds of Mars (with Warren Hammond)

Denver Moon: The Saint of Mars (with Warren Hammond)

GRAPHIC NOVELS

Denver Moon: Metamorphosis (with Warren Hammond and Aaron Lovett)

Tooth and Claw (with Angie Hodapp and Aaron Lovett)

ANTHOLOGIES (Edited)

Nightmares Unhinged: Twenty Tales of Terror

Cyber World: Tales of Humanity's Tomorrow (with Jason Heller)

Georgetown Haunts and Mysteries (with Jeanne C. Stein)

Blood Business: Crime Stories from this World and Beyond (with Mario Acevedo)

Psi-Wars: Classified Cases of Psychic Phenomena

It Came from the Multiplex: 80s Midnight Chillers

www.ingramcontent.com/pod-product-compliance
Lightning Source LLC
Chambersburg PA
CBHW010645100726
47900CB00011B/2972